The Walkathon

Story by Jan Weeks
Illustrations by Pat Reynolds

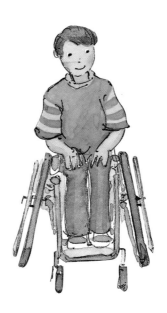

My name is Peter, and I use a wheelchair to get around. I can do a lot of things in my wheelchair, and this year I want to be in the School Walkathon.

At the Walkathon last year, Mrs. Hunt let me help hand out the oranges and drinks to the walkers. The teachers and parents said I was an expert and that they couldn't have managed without me. But handing out oranges isn't the same as doing laps.

"Are you going to give out drinks and oranges again this year?" my friend Michael asked.

"I suppose so," I said. "But I really wish I could push myself around the course, doing laps with you."

"The path is a bit bumpy," said Michael.

"And I couldn't manage the sloping part," I said, gloomily.

Sometimes being in a wheelchair is no fun at all. Other times it's not so bad. I'm really good at moving the wheels around. I can catch and throw, so Michael and I often play with a ball. Michael makes sure I'm not left out of things.

"If I get the mystery prize," said Michael, "I'll share it with you."

Mrs. Hunt has taught us for nearly two years, and last year she gave a mystery prize to the person in our class who walked the most laps. Olivia won it.

"What's the prize going to be this year?" Michael asked Mrs. Hunt.

Mrs. Hunt laughed. "It's a **mystery**," she said. "When you've won it, you'll know."

"There's no way I can possibly win it," I said to Michael.

"Peter really wants to be in the Walkathon this year," Michael told Mrs. Hunt.

Mrs. Hunt looked at me. "It's not a good course for a wheelchair," she said. "Some of the ground is uneven, and the hilly part would be too difficult."

"I know," I said.

"But I could push Peter over the hard parts," said Michael. "Would you let me? That way we could both be in the Walkathon."

"I'll think about it," promised Mrs. Hunt. "It's not a bad idea, but it would be hard work on the slope."

That afternoon, Mrs. Hunt called a class meeting. Michael told everyone about his idea.

"Michael needn't do all the pushing," said Olivia. "We could all take turns. That way no one would get too tired."

"That's a good idea," said Mrs. Hunt. "Who would like to help Peter in the Walkathon?"

Everyone said they would take a turn.

"But you'll have to get permission, Peter," said Mrs. Hunt. "You can ask your parents tonight. I'll write them a note."

Mom and Dad liked the idea. "You've got a good sturdy wheelchair," said Mom.

"And your arms are strong enough," said Dad. "You'll be able to push yourself some of the way."

I called all our friends and everyone said they would sponsor me. I felt great. If I finished even one lap I would earn a lot of money for the school — and maybe I would be able to finish more than one!

The night before the Walkathon, I was so excited it was hard to get to sleep.

When we went into the school, Mrs. Hunt told us all what we had to do when the Walkathon began.

"I shall be sitting at a long table by the school gate," she said. "Every time you finish a lap, you must report to me. I'll put a stamp on your sponsor card. Don't forget!"

At last we were all allowed to go outside.

I pushed myself along the flat ground toward the gate. Michael walked beside me, and we waited until it was Room Four's turn to go.

Then Mrs. Hunt gave us the signal and we were off. I turned the wheels around and around as fast as I could. I kept up with Michael for the first part of the course, before we came to the hilly part.

Michael started to push me up the slope. Olivia was waiting halfway up. "My turn now," she said, as she took over from Michael, who was puffing.

Soon it seemed that everyone in the class wanted to push me!

When we came back to the school gate at the end of the first lap, I took a piece of orange. Then Mrs. Hunt stamped my card.

With all the help my friends were giving me, it was easy to keep going. I did a second lap — and another.

Every time I went past the long table by the school gate, Mrs. Hunt asked me if I was getting tired. "No way!" I said. I wanted to do as many laps as I could, even though the wheelchair bumped and jolted for some of the way.

It was fun doing the Walkathon with my friends, and I had a lot of stamps on my sponsor card. But I was tired by the end. It was good to get out of my chair and go to bed that night!

The next day in class, Mrs. Hunt said, "It's time to announce the winner of the mystery prize for the Walkathon. The person who did the most laps was… Peter!"

"Here's the mystery envelope," said Mrs. Hunt, handing it to me. "Good effort, Peter!"

"Great!" I thought. "Thanks, Mrs. Hunt." I opened the envelope and pulled out a voucher. It came from *The Sports Shop*.

I looked at all the things I had won, and started to read aloud:

1 large rubber ball, 2 sets of jacks... "Wow!" I thought. "Michael and I could have fun with those!" The list went on... *2 yo-yos, 3 tennis balls, a bat and glove...*

But then I remembered that everyone in the class had helped me. If they hadn't slowed down and pushed me up the hilly part, they might have done more laps themselves. Michael or Olivia might have won the prize if they hadn't kept stopping to help me.

I told Mrs. Hunt that the whole class had helped me win.

"So I want everyone to share the prize," I said. "Let's keep all the stuff in our classroom. Then we can all have some fun!"

And that's what we did.